The Princess and the Pea

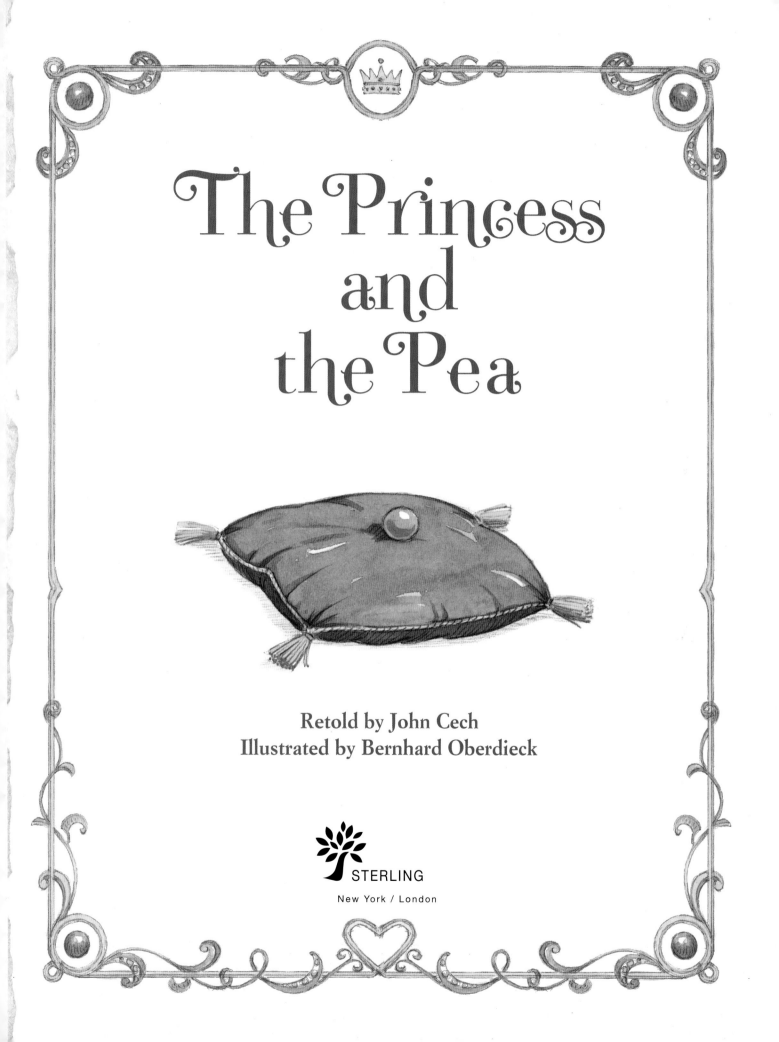

Retold by John Cech
Illustrated by Bernhard Oberdieck

STERLING
New York / London

STERLING and the distinctive Sterling logo are
registered trademarks of Sterling Publishing Co., Inc

Library of Congress Cataloging-in-Publication Data

Cech, John.
The princess and the pea / by Hans Christian Andersen ;
retold by John Cech ; illustrated by Bernhard Oberdieck.
p. cm.
Summary: An abridgement of the tale in which a girl proves that
she is a real princess by feeling a pea through twenty mattresses and twenty
featherbeds. Includes historical notes about Hans
Christian Andersen and the original fairy tale.
ISBN 978-1-4027-3065-8
[1. Fairy tales.] I. Oberdieck, Bernhard, ill. II. Andersen, H. C.
(Hans Christian), 1805–1875.
Prindsessen paa ærten. English. III. Title.

PZ8.B5595Pr 2007
[E]—dc22

2006007033

6   8   10   9   7

Published by Sterling Publishing Co., Inc.
387 Park Avenue South, New York, NY 10016
Text © 2007 by John Cech
Illustrations © 2007 by Bernhard Oberdieck
Distributed in Canada by Sterling Publishing
c/o Canadian Manda Group, 165 Dufferin Street,
Toronto, Ontario, Canada M6K 3H6
Distributed in the United Kingdom by GMC Distribution Services,
Castle Place, 166 High Street, Lewes, East Sussex, England BN7 1XU
Distributed in Australia by Capricorn Link (Australia) Pty. Ltd.
P.O. Box 704, Windsor, NSW 2756, Australia

Design by Josh Simons, Simonsays Design!

Printed in China 4/2013
All rights reserved

Sterling ISBN 978-1-4027-3065-8

For information about custom editions, special sales, premium and
corporate purchases, please contact Sterling Special Sales
Department at 800-805-5489 or specialsales@sterlingpublishing.com.

A long time ago, there lived a prince who was looking for someone very special to marry. But that someone had to be a real princess. The prince met lots of young ladies who wanted to marry him. Some of them were very pretty, some were very rich, and some were very smart. But none of them was a real princess. And so he kept looking, and hoping, and yearning.

The prince wore out his shoes dancing with all the eligible young ladies. He wore himself out going to parties with them, and he talked with them until he was so tired that he couldn't talk anymore. But still, he couldn't find a real princess.

"Perhaps," said the king, "there are no more real princesses."

"Maybe," said the queen, "all the real princesses have already found their princes. Besides, dear son, you know you are very, very picky."

And so it went—more parties and dances and conversations— for another year. Until one night, in the middle of a ferocious thunderstorm, there was a knock at the door of the castle.

The king was up late (the thunder had awakened him, you see), and so he went to the door.

Outside stood a young woman. She was soaking wet.

"Please give me shelter," she implored.

The worried king asked how she came to be alone in the night.

"My family and I were traveling through the forest. It was so dark and stormy that we lost each other. I walked until I saw the light in the castle."

By now the queen, too, had awakened. She took the young woman with her to a guest room to give her dry clothing and to settle her in for the night.

"Who is your family?" asked the queen.

"I am a king's daughter, though you wouldn't know it to look at me," the young woman said. Indeed, her clothes were torn and muddy, and her face was weary from traveling.

Hmmm, thought the queen. *We'll soon see if she's a real princess. Real princesses are very, very sensitive.*

nd so the queen called the maids and the footmen and ordered them to bring twenty mattresses and twenty feather comforters to the bedroom. "Just stack them up high," she told them. "We want our guest to be comfortable after her ordeal."

While a warm bath was being prepared, the servants piled up mattresses and feather comforters until they nearly reached the ceiling. Then they set a ladder next to the bed so their guest could climb up.

After the servants left, the queen took one small, green pea that she had gotten from the kitchen and tucked it as far under the bottom mattress as her arm could reach.

When the young visitor was ready for bed, the queen helped her climb the ladder to the top of the stack of mattresses and comforters, blew out the candle, and wished her a good night and pleasant dreams.

In the morning, when the young woman awoke and joined the royal family for breakfast, the queen asked her how she had slept.

"Oh, I barely slept a wink last night," she replied. "I must have strained my back in the forest, because it felt like I was sleeping on a stone and not on the stack of mattresses and feather comforters that you prepared for me."

The queen knew at once that this must be a real princess. She wanted to tell her son about her test, but she could not get his attention. He was gazing lovingly into the eyes of the princess, and she into his, and they were both smiling.

After breakfast, the king showed the princess around the castle while his men searched the forest for her family to bring them safely to the shelter of the palace.

When the queen was finally alone with the prince, she said to him, "I think she's the one, son." Then she told him about placing the pea under the stack of their guest's mattresses. "Only a real princess would have felt a pea in that bed," she said.

"Thank you, Mother," said the prince. "But I didn't need a pea to tell me she is a real princess. I could see it in the gentleness of her eyes, hear it in the softness of her voice, and feel it in the kindness of her heart."

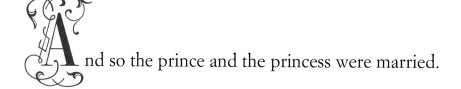

And so the prince and the princess were married.

Now, you might be asking, whatever became of the pea?
Well, some say the pea was put into a museum, others
say the pea was cooked in the prince and princess's wedding
soup. But still others say the queen kept it to remind herself
of her son's wisdom in recognizing his real princess.

Historical Note

Born in 1805, Hans Christian Andersen grew up in the small Danish town of Odense, among the poorest of the poor. Some of the few glimmers of light in his otherwise grim childhood were the stories that his grandmother told. These would later make him famous, just as a gypsy fortune teller had once predicted to his mother. Shortly before he left Odense to try his fortunes in the big city of Copenhagen, Andersen's mother took him to visit the town's seer. "First you have to suffer a great deal," the gypsy told him, "and then you become famous." And suffer he did. Yet these hardships ended up providing him with the basic material for what would become his most famous story, "The Ugly Duckling." In fact, Andersen would write of this story and others in his autobiography, *The Fairy Tale of My Life*: "Every character is taken from life; every one of them; not one of them is invented. I know and have known them all."

"The Princess and the Pea" was among the first of Hans Christian Andersen's tales to appear, and has since become one of his most popular. This story, along with three others, was originally published just before Christmas of 1835 in Copenhagen, Denmark, in a small book called *Fairy Tales, Told for Children*. Andersen said of these first four works:

"I wrote the stories for children, but older people ought to find them worth listening to." He went on to note that "The Princess and the Pea" was a tale he "had heard as a child, either in the spinning room or during the harvesting of the hops."

According to folklore scholars, "The Princess and the Pea" most likely traveled to Denmark from Sweden, where there are versions of the story that are very similar to Andersen's. In an Italian folktale, the princess is kept awake by a wrinkle in the sheet, and in a very old tale from Kashmir, a noble young man feels a single hair under seven mattresses. That those who are truly "royal" possess extraordinary sensitivities is, of course, quite an ancient idea and one that still exists today. And the possibility that the "real princess" may be disguised as the most unlikely maiden continues to be the subject of any number of stories, television shows, and movies.

Andersen wrote: "In a little land like ours, the poet is always poor; honor, therefore, is the golden bird he tries to grasp. Time will tell whether I can catch it by telling fairy tales." To judge by the continuing popularity of "The Princess and the Pea," and of many of Andersen's other stories, he certainly has caught that "golden bird."